THE MARKET LADY AND THE MANGO TREE

The Market Lady and the Mango Tree

PETE and MARY WATSON

Tambourine Books  New York

For those wonderful people who read to us when
we were young, and for their grandchildren P.W.

For my mother, my most severe critic, greatest
admirer, and dearest friend M.W.

Printed in Singapore. Book design by Golda Laurens. The text
type is printed in Cloister Old Style.

Library of Congress Cataloging in Publication Data

Watson, Pete, 1948-   The Market Lady and the mango tree/by
Pete Watson; illustrated by Mary Watson.—1st ed. p. cm. Sum-
mary: A sly merchant gets rich when she devises a contraption
for collecting mangoes, but a dream teaches her a lesson about
greed. [1. Mango—Fiction. 2. Greed—Fiction. 3. Africa—
Fiction.] I. Watson, Mary, 1953- ill. II Title. PZ7.W3286
Mar1994 [E]—dc20 93-7725 CIP AC
ISBN 0-688-12970-6 (trade).—ISBN 0-688-12971-4 (lib.)
10 9 8 7 6 5 4 3 2 1
First edition

Market Lady sits big in the cool shade of a mango tree.

She sits big beside candy-fat jars and tall stacks of crackers. She sits big behind baskets and bowls of good things to eat, like melons, bananas, and sugar-dipped dates…coconuts, oranges, and big purple grapes.

Around crowd the children, little barefoot children with eyes as bright as diamonds and arms as skinny as twigs. Having no money to buy what they see, they wait for mangoes to fall from the tree.

Pineapple 10¢

Mangoes are sweeter than candy when they ripen in the sun. So it's wonderful fun for the children to wait…and to scramble and tumble and wrestle and race when the mangoes drop down from the tree with a thump.

Tick-tick-ker-plunk! go the mangoes when the wind blows the leaves and the afternoon breeze whistles them down to the ground by the dozen.

Click-click-crack! goes a big juicy mango that falls on the mat where Market Lady sits in the cool shade.

"Hey! Come back!" yelled the woman when a mango rolled off her mat and into the sand where a child no bigger than a whistle reached out her hand and said, "Hurray! A mango for me!"

"That mango is mine!" cried Market Lady. "You bring it back or I'll have your hide!"

But everyone knew that the law of the tree is that once they have fallen, mangoes are free.

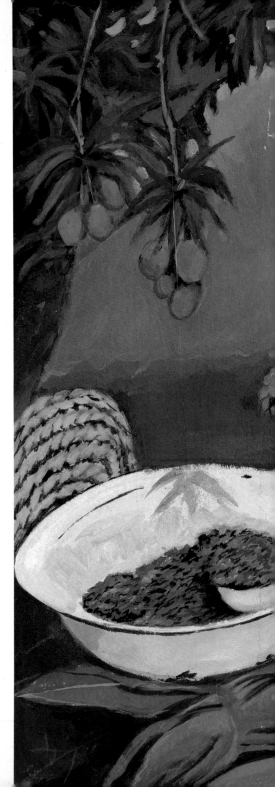

5/25¢

So Market Lady, clever merchant that she was, decided to stop the mangoes from falling. In the branches above her, she arranged a large net. It hung like a funnel over her mat. She called her invention a mango trap.

The breeze blew hot and every eye watched when—*tick-tick-zip!*—a mango knocked its way down through the leaves. Nobody moved or scrambled or jumped when the mango hit with a gentle bump, right in Market Lady's lap.

The children did not want to accuse her of stealing their mangoes. They just planned in a whisper to sneak up behind and to loosen the net so a few mangoes might fall to the ground. But she was wide as the trunk where she leaned her great back, and with one eye half open, she swatted and screeched when anything moved or when anything squeaked.

Later that day, Market Lady made a big sign that said MANGOES FOR SALE—1¢ EACH. And when she counted the money she made in a week, she decided to make a trap in every mango tree in the marketplace.

With the money she made from her poaching and plunder, she purchased a big, black, beautiful Mercedes Benz. It had a shiny hood and whitewall tires and a horn that went *beega-beega-beega*.

Every day when the hustle and bustle of the market was over, she filled up the Benz with mangoes and money and assorted junk that fell from the trees. You know the sort: old bird nests and kites and old tires from bikes and slingshots and hats and even a monkey that was taking a nap. When the trunk was full, she put the rest on the roof. And then she was gone.

Where did she go with her carload of mangoes? To a factory island where they made mango jelly. To reach it she had to cross a lagoon on a rickety bridge that swayed in the moonlight. It gave her such shivers and quivers, she sometimes wondered if it was wrong to do what she was doing.

But she never wondered long. The price of her mangoes rose to two cents apiece, then to three, four, and five cents—well out of reach of most of the people in the marketplace. Finally, only the rich jellymakers could afford to buy her mangoes.

One night, she dreamed about mangoes—the biggest kind, which she loaded in wagons attached behind the Benz like freight-train cars. When she pulled seven great wagons and could pull no more, she came to a wide river where bronze hippos wallowed on a mud bank in the sunset glow.

Knowing quite well the danger the hippos posed to her cargo, Market Lady made a sweeping turn toward the south and stepped on the gas.

But the hippos were already upon the caravan. They were running alongside and bumping the carts so that the mangoes bounced down from the piles into their wide, waiting mouths.

Chew they did not, the ravenous beasts. The mangoes rolled down past their great hippo teeth, into the depths of their hollow-brown throats.

"Thank goodness!" she cried when a rickety bridge appeared and she swung the caravan onto its noisy planks.

But already many of the hippos were riding in the wagons, and many more jostled along behind.

The bridge began to creak and crack. It swung and shuddered, and with a terrible snap, broke in two, spilling mangoes and hippos into the muddy waters below.

Market Lady tossed and turned in a pool of riverbed sweat as a school of mangofish nibbled at her toes. She shivered and shook and desperately looked for her Benz.

But it was gone, all gone, except for one clue—a small, wooden sign that floated by just as she awoke.

MANGOES, it said. $5 FOR 2.

That's what changed her, the children say. She sold the Benz that very day. She tore down her signs and demolished her traps.

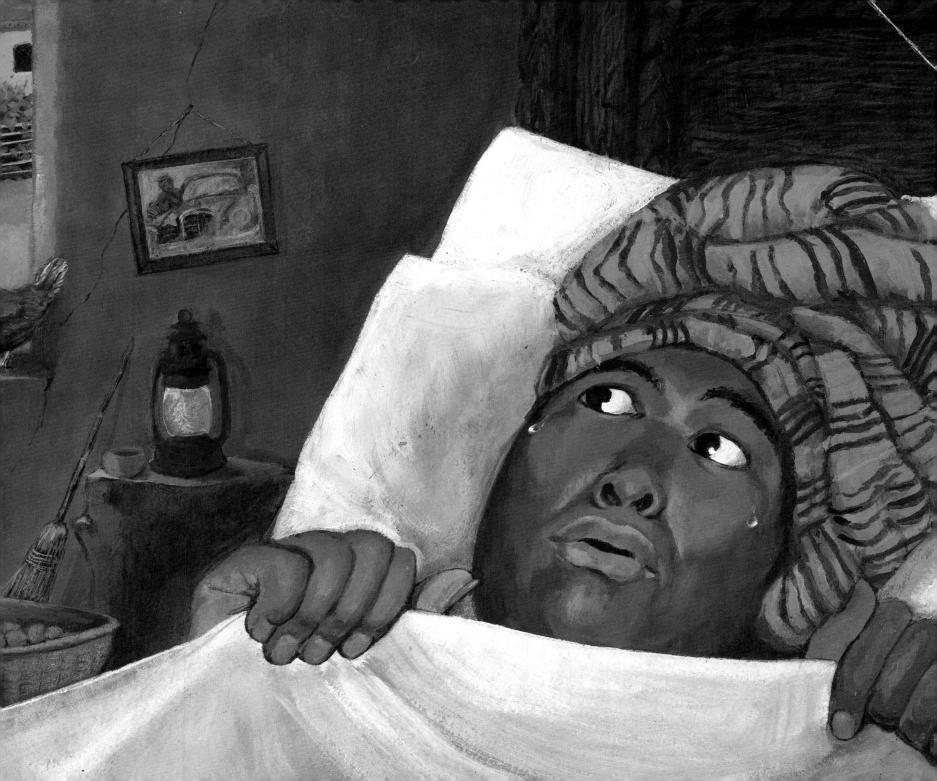

And gave everyone mangoes straight from her lap. Then she stood up and explained that the change in her prices was caused by a crisis that was caused by a hippopotamus that no one could see.

"Which means," she said, "that you can't earn a living by selling what's free."